Wonder Walkers

Dedicated to Leyla, mi amiga buena

Nancy Paulsen Books
An imprint of Penguin Random House LLC, New York

Nancy Paulsen Books is a trademark of Penguin Random House LLC. • Visit us online at penguinrandomhouse.com • Library of Congress Cataloging-in-Publication Data | Names: Archer, Micha, author, illustrator. | Title: Wonder walkers / Micha Archer. | Description: New York: Nancy Paulsen Books, [2021] | Summary: "Two curious children go for a walk, asking imaginative questions about the natural beauty that surrounds them"—Provided by publisher. | Identifiers: LCCN 2020019300 | ISBN 9780593109649 (hardcover) | ISBN 9780593109663 (ebook) | ISBN 9780593109656 (ebook) | Subjects: CYAC: Nature—Fiction. | Classification: LCC PZ7.1.A728 Wo 2021 | DDC [E]—dc23 | LC record available at https://lccn.loc.gov/2020019300 • Manufactured in China by RR Donnelley Asia Printing Solutions Ltd. • ISBN 9780593109649 • 10 9 8 7 6 5 4 3 2 1 • Design by Eileen Savage. Text set in a song for jennifer. • The illustrations were done in inks and collage, using tissue paper and patterned papers created with homemade stamps.

Micha Archer

Wonder Walkers

Nancy Paulsen Books

Wonder walk?

Sure.

Is the sun the
world's light bulb?

Is fog the river's blanket?

Do mountains have bones?
Are forests the mountain's fur?

I wonder.

Me too.

Are
trees
the sky's
legs?

Are branches trees' arms?

Is dirt the world's skin?

Are roots the plant's toes?

Do caves have mouths?

Are shells the shore's necklace?
Is the ocean the world's bath?

Are rivers the
earth's veins?

Is the wind the
world breathing?

Is rain the day's tears?

Is the moon the world's night-light?

I wonder.

Me too.